Harry Help-a-lot

Irene Howat

for Harry and Malcolm

Christian Focus Publications

Harry's nickname was Harry Help-a-lot. He just loved to help.

Harry and his yellow canary lived at number 10 Main Street.

Harry called his canary Cheery Boy because his whistling cheered everyone up.

10

When the bathroom flooded at number 8, Mary yelled, 'Quick! Get Harry Help-a-lot!'

Harry mended the sink.
'I like helping,' he said.

Fred at Number 6 took out his bike and found it had a puncture. 'I'll get Harry Help-a-lot,' he told his wife.

Harry came and fixed the puncture. 'I like helping,' he told Cheery Boy.

Jill at number 9 was crying.

'My toy train's broken,' she wept.
'I'll phone for Harry Help-a-lot,'
her mum said.

Harry came and
fixed Jill's train.

'I like helping,' he
told Cheery Boy.

Malcolm at number 7 was cleaning his chimney. 'I need someone to go on the roof,' he said. 'I'll ask Harry Help-a-lot.'

Harry climbed on to the roof and watched for the chimney brush coming up.

That's when it happened. Harry Help-a-lot slipped and slithered, clattered then crashed right off the roof into Malcolm's garden. He hurt his left arm, his right leg and his big toe. Poor Harry Help-a-lot!

'I've brought your dinner,' Mary said, after Harry was back home. 'And I've brought your paper,' Fred told him.

'I don't like having to be helped,' Harry sighed to Cheery Boy.

'I've come to help,' said Jill. 'Would you like to play Snakes and Ladders?'

'Yes please,' Harry told his young friend.

'It's lovely being helped,' Harry told Cheery Boy, when Jill left for home.

Cheery Boy whistled and sang, then flew on to Harry Help-a-lot's shoulder.

'Your singing has cheered me up,' Harry told the bird. 'Imagine Harry Help-a-lot being helped by his own canary.'

Dear Father in heaven,

thank you for helping me, and for all the people who help me too. Please help me to be more like Jesus who is always helping people.

Amen.

'Dear children, let us not love with words or tongue
but with actions and in truth.'
1 John 3:18

'Carry each others burdens, and in this way you will
fulfil the law of Christ.'
Galatians 6:2

Collect the Little Lots Series
and answer these questions

Lucy Lie-a-lot

Where are the goldfish
called Round and About?

Harry Help-a-lot

What does Cheery Boy
the canary like to do?

Bobby Boast-a-lot

Is Champion the bravest
dog around?

Granny Grump-a-lot

How many mice has
Hunter the cat caught?

Lorna Look-a-lot

What interesting thing
has Sniff the dog found?

William Work-a-lot

How did Stuff the
hamster get his name?

Published by Christian Focus Publications,
Geanies House, Fearn, Tain, Ross-shire, IV20 1TW, Scotland.
www.christianfocus.com © Copyright 2005 Irene Howat Illustrated by Michel de Boer * Printed in the U.K.
The Little Lots series looks at positive and negative characteristics and values.
These titles will help children understand what God wants from our everyday lives. Other titles in this series include:
Lucy Lie-a-lot, Granny Grump-a-lot, Lorna Look-a-lot, William Work-a-lot, Bobby Boast-a-lot